MISS NELSON IS MISSING!

HARRY ALLARD
JAMES MARSHALL

HOUGHTON MIFFLIN HARCOURT
BOSTON NEW YORK

For My Sister Jacqueline
—H.A.
For Nedd Takahashi
—J.M.

Library of Congress Cataloging in Publication Data
Allard, Harry.
  Miss Nelson is missing!

  SUMMARY: The kids in Room 207 take advantage of their
teacher's good nature until she disappears and they are
faced with a vile substitute.
  [1. School stories. 2. Behavior--Fiction]
I. Marshall, James, 1942-   II. Title.
PZ7.A413Mi   [E]   76-55918
ISBN 0-395-25296-2

Printed in China

ISBN-13 978-0-395-25296-3 Hardcover
ISBN-13 978-0-395-40146-0 Paperback

SCP 85 84 83 82 81 80 79
4500707672

The kids in Room 207 were misbehaving again.

Spitballs stuck to the ceiling.

Paper planes whizzed through the air.

They were the worst-behaved class in the whole school.

"Now settle down," said Miss Nelson in a sweet voice.

But the class would *not* settle down.

They whispered and giggled.

They squirmed and made faces.

They were even rude during story hour.

And they always refused to do their lessons.

"Something will have to be done," said Miss Nelson.

The next morning Miss Nelson did not come to school.
"Wow!" yelled the kids. "Now we can *really* act up!"
They began to make more spitballs and paper planes.
"Today let's be just terrible!" they said.

"Not so fast!" hissed an unpleasant voice.

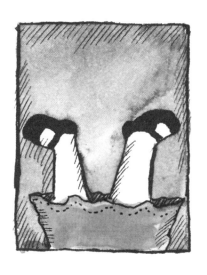

A woman in an ugly black dress stood before them.

"I am your new teacher, Miss Viola Swamp."

And she rapped the desk with her ruler.

"Where is Miss Nelson?" asked the kids.

"Never mind that!" snapped Miss Swamp. "Open those arithmetic books!"

Miss Nelson's kids did as they were told.

They could see that Miss Swamp was a real witch.

She meant business.

Right away she put them to work.

And she loaded them down with homework.

"We'll have no story hour today," said Miss Swamp.

"Keep your mouths shut," said Miss Swamp.

"Sit perfectly still," said Miss Swamp.

"And if you misbehave, you'll be sorry," said
Miss Swamp.

The kids in Room 207 had *never* worked so hard.

Days went by and there was no sign of Miss Nelson.
The kids *missed* Miss Nelson!

"Maybe we should try to find her," they said.

Some of them went to the police.

Detective McSmogg was assigned to the case.

He listened to their story.

He scratched his chin.

"Hmmmm," he said. "Hmmm."

"I think Miss Nelson is missing."

Detective McSmogg would
not be much help.

Other kids went to Miss Nelson's house.

The shades were tightly drawn, and no one answered the door.

In fact, the only person they *did* see was the wicked Miss Viola Swamp, coming up the street.

"If she sees us, she'll give us more homework."

They got away just in time.

Maybe something *terrible* happened to Miss Nelson!

"Maybe she was gobbled up by a shark!" said one of the kids.

But that didn't seem likely.

SHARKS
(VERY UNPLEASANT)

"Maybe Miss Nelson went to Mars!" said another kid.
But that didn't seem likely either.

"I know!" exclaimed one know-it-all. "Maybe Miss Nelson's
car was carried off by a swarm of angry butterflies!"
But that was the least likely of all.

The kids in Room 207 became very discouraged.

It seemed that Miss Nelson was never coming back.

And they would be stuck with Miss Viola Swamp forever.

They heard footsteps in the hall.

"Here comes the witch," they whispered.

"Hello, children," someone said in a sweet voice.

It was Miss Nelson!

"Did you miss me?" she asked.

"We certainly did!" cried all the kids.

"Where were you?"

"That's my little secret," said Miss Nelson.

"How about a story hour?"

"Oh yes!" cried the kids.

Miss Nelson noticed that during story hour no one
was rude or silly.

"What brought about this lovely change?" she asked.

"That's *our* little secret," said the kids.

Back home Miss Nelson took off her coat and hung it
in the closet (right next to an ugly black dress).
When it was time for bed she sang a little song.
"I'll never tell," she said to herself with a smile.

P.S. Detective McSmogg is working on a new case.
He is *now* looking for Miss Viola Swamp.